Story by Lisa Lucas
Pictures by Laurie Stein

For information regarding permission, write to:
Mehta Publishing: info@mehtapublishers.com

All rights reserved.
This edition published in India by Mehta Publishers
www.mehtapublishers.com

Printed in India by Mehta Offset

First Edition

Simon loves clocks.

He l ves the numbers. He l ves the faces.

M st of all,
he l ves
the s und they
make...
tick t ck tick t ck.

But Simon doesn't know how to tell time.
So he's late for almost everything...

bowling,

and birthdays,

and...

always the bus.

His mother tells him
to "hurry up" a lot.

Simon doesn't like that.

His big sister Ruth stomps her feet when she says it.

"Hurry up!"

Simon really doesn't like that.

And even Grandma Anna says it to him...
sometimes harshly...when she's awake.

"Hurry up!"

One day, Simon's mother says, "Tomorrow we are going to the fair. There is going to be a special clown show that we don't want to miss."

"If you're not ready,
we're leaving you behind.

Well...with Grandma Anna."

Simon wants to go to the fair.
He wants to see the clowns.

He doesn't know what to do.

So
he
thinks
for
awhile...

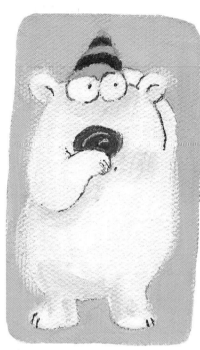

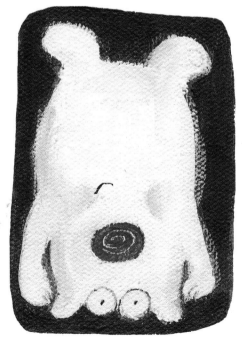
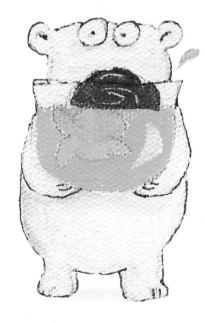

...and thinks some more.

"I know", he says.

"I need my clocks. And I need some help!"

Ruth sets the alarms.
It takes awhile.

Once they are all set, Simon shuts the door,
turns off the light and sits on his bed.

Listening to the steady
TICK TOCK TICK TOCK
beat makes him feel in charge.

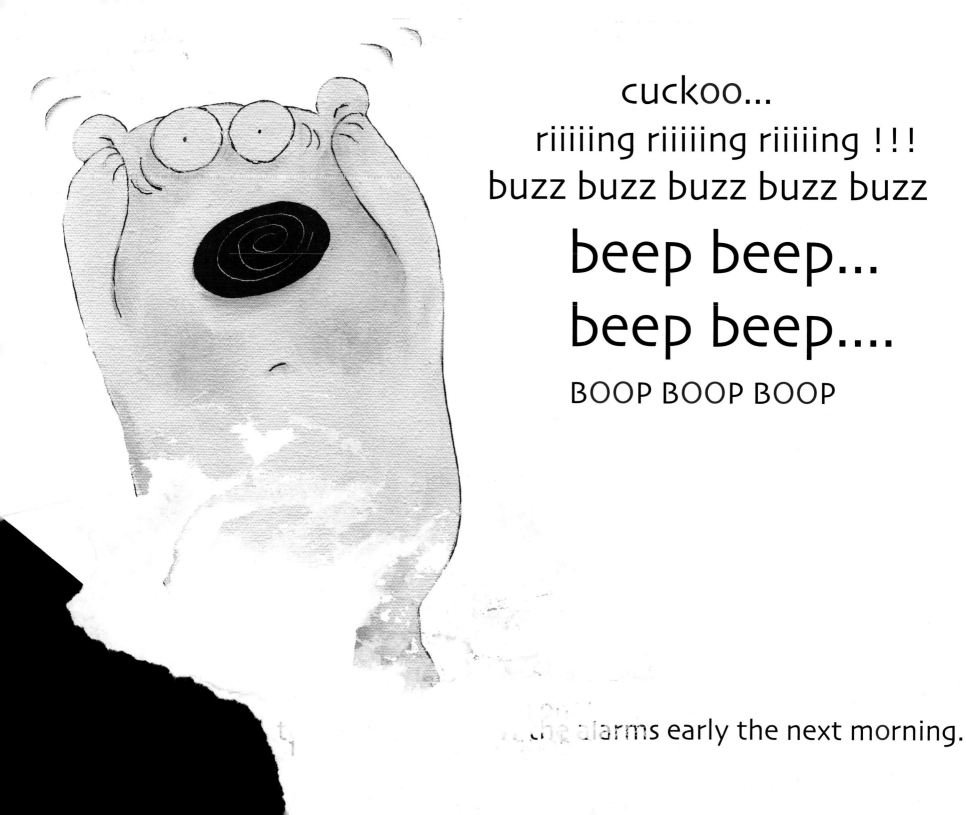

cuckoo...
riiiiing riiiiing riiiiing !!!
buzz buzz buzz buzz buzz

beep beep...
beep beep....

BOOP BOOP BOOP

...the alarms early the next morning.

He gets out of bed. He gets himself ready and runs to the front door.

He has gon
He waits at the door

There isn't a sound.
Simon cries out,
"Hey Mom....
Mom...
Where are you?"

There is silence.

With all those clocks, how could he be late again?

Have they left without him?

He starts to cry.

Simon cries **louder** and

louder and even

louder.

All of a sudden,
he hears his mother's voice,

"Simon, is that you? What time is it? I can't believe I slept in."

They finally arrive at the fair.
They're a little late for the clown show.

But that's OK.

They're the last to leave.

LISA LUCAS

Lisa has always been surrounded with kids. She has them. She teaches them. She reads to them, and now writes for them. For the last 9 years, she has taught Special Education in inner city schools promoting community partnerships and setting up programs for emerging and intermediate readers. She has also written for Reader's Digest and freelanced for several newspapers. Lisa has joined forces with her longtime high school friend and illustrator, Laurie Stein, and together they are cooking up a batch of stories.

LAURIE STEIN

Laurie has been drawing ever since she could hold a crayon. As a three year old she took a crayon and scribbled her way up the staircase when her family moved to a new home. Since then, she has learned to draw on paper and canvas and has substituted that crayon for paints and pastels. Her drawings fill many children's books and her paintings hang in a number of homes across North America. She collaborates with her lifelong author/friend Lisa Lucas and they have a whole library of books waiting to be read aloud. You can see more of Laurie's work at www.lauriestein.com